First U.S. edition 2019

Library of Congress Catalog Card Number pending
ISBN 978-1-5362-1230-3

19 20 21 22 23 24 TLF 10 9 8 7 6 5 4 3 2

Printed in Dongguan, Guangdong, China

This book was typeset in Kosmik and DK Black Bamboo.
The illustrations were created digitally.

Candlewick Entertainment
an imprint of
Candlewick Press
99 Dover Street
Somerville, Massachusetts 02144

visit us at www.candlewick.com

THE STORY OF GIGANTOSAURUS™

CANDLEWICK
ENTERTAINMENT

GIGANTOSAURUS

Once upon a time in the Cretaceous world, millions of years ago, dinosaurs roamed the earth. They were the most massive creatures that ever existed. With their pointy claws, sharp teeth, and fearsome roars, these creatures were TERRIFYING . . .

well, most of them.

I must write that down in my Gigantopedia!

I'm a para . . . a parasolo . . . a dinosaur!

Mazu was a curious young ankylosaurus who loved to learn new things. Whenever she discovered a new fact, she'd write it in her trusty Gigantopedia.

Rocky, a little parasaurolophus, was always looking for new adventures. He certainly wasn't afraid of a little danger—he'd usually run toward it!

I may be tiny, but I'm TOUGH!

Unlike Rocky, Bill was a nervous dinosaur. Even though he'd one day grow into a HUGE brachiosaurus, he was nowhere near as fearless as his friends.

Where am I?

Tiny was a triceratops who loved having fun.
She could usually be found drawing,
singing, and making friends.

Although the four friends were very different,
they always had a great time together. They made musical
instruments with bamboo, went swinging on jungle vines,
and snacked on tasty coconuts all day.

All in all, they had a pretty
great life. There was just one
thing that could ruin their day . . .

GIGANTOSAURUS!

He was the largest, most dangerous dinosaur in the whole of the Cretaceous world, and he was ALWAYS hungry.

The dinos were terrified of Gigantosaurus, but they were also fascinated by him. What was his favorite thing to do? Where did he hang out? What did he like to eat? (Hopefully not baby dinos!)

All they knew for sure was that at the sound of Giganto's stomps, you had to . . .

One day, Mazu had an idea. "Let's go Gigantosaurus hunting," she suggested. "We can finally find out where he hides away all day!"

Tiny and Rocky were very excited. Bill, on the other hand, wasn't so sure.

No way! He's just too scary!

But Mazu was determined. She armed her friends with some handy tools for their adventure—a leafy spyglass, a sundial, and some coconuts (Giganto hunting was thirsty work!). Soon they were ready to go.

They headed to the deepest part of the jungle—the perfect hiding place for a MASSIVE dinosaur.

"This would be a great spot for Giganto to get some peace and quiet!" said Mazu thoughtfully.

"Then is it really the best idea to disturb him?" Bill asked, trembling with fear.

Let's just go home!

"Hey, look up there!" Tiny said, excitedly pointing up at a shape through the trees. They crept forward to get a closer look.

"Oh no," Mazu said. "It's only Archie the archaeopteryx."

What do you mean "ONLY"?

Determined, Mazu led her friends out of the jungle and into the savanna. With its fiery lava, the volcano up ahead seemed like an ideal spot for a TERRIFYING dinosaur to spend his days.

"I bet Giganto thinks we'd be way too scared to disturb him there!" Mazu said.

The young dinosaurs followed eagerly. Even Bill was starting to feel excited that they might finally find Gigantosaurus's hangout.

The friends spotted a figure in the distance and slowly made their way closer. But this time, they ran into Dilo the dilophosaurus.

Sorry! No Giganto here.

They were tired and hungry, and starting to think they'd never find Gigantosaurus.

"You can't give up now!" Mazu cried. So the dinosaurs trudged on to the lake.

We are not quitters!

At the lake, all was calm—until suddenly, the enormous Terminonator lunged out of the water toward the little dinos! She opened her mouth and revealed her huge spiky teeth.

ARGHHH!

The dinosaurs ran and ran until they were safely back in the jungle. "We ran away too quickly to learn much about him, but I did discover something about Giganto. . . ." Mazu said happily as she wrote in her Gigantopedia.

He has REALLY smelly breath.